Killing
Mum

Killing
Mum

Allan Guthrie

CRIME EXPRESS

Essex County Council Libraries

Killing Mum
by Allan Guthrie

Published by Crime Express in 2009
Crime Express is an imprint of
Five Leaves Publications,
PO Box 8786, Nottingham NG1 9AW
www.fiveleaves.co.uk

Copyright ©Allan Guthrie, 2009

ISBN: 978 1 905512 69 0

Crime Express 8

Five Leaves acknowledges financial support
from Arts Council England

Five Leaves is a member of Inpress
(www.inpressbooks.co.uk),
representing independent publishers.

Design and typeset by Four Sheets
Printed in Great Britain by the MPG Books Group,
Bodmin and King's Lynn

1

The padded envelope contained a note and a bundle of cash. The note read:

> *Charlie —*
> *Advance for Valerie Anderson. You know her address. Second half of payment on completion of job.*

It wasn't signed.

Carlos Morales counted the cash. He counted it again. Ten thousand pounds. He stuffed the money back in the envelope and placed it on the counter.

He was alone in the tanning studio today, which was just as well. He snaked out from behind the counter, grabbed the nearest rack and pulled it over. It crashed to the floor, crushing tubs of tanning lotion and beauty products that burst and spewed and leaked all over the previously squeaky clean floor.

"*Mierda*," he said, out of habit.

He stepped over the debris, walked to the door, locked it, switched the sign to 'closed'.

He slid his mobile out of his pocket and called home.

Maggie answered. "What's wrong?" she said.

"Just wanted to see how you were."

"At ten past nine? What's wrong, Charlie?"

There it was, the name on the note. He couldn't bring himself to think it might be her. There had to be some other explanation. Other people called him Charlie. Well, one other person.

He breathed in. Hadn't had a cigarette in ten months, but when he dreamed, he always had a fag in his hand. He wished he was dreaming right now. "How's my little girl?"

"She's fine, misses her daddy."

"Tell her to hang on. I'm closing up. I'll be there in twenty minutes."

***

Carlos climbed in his car, got the engine purring, thumbed through his CDs and couldn't find anything he wanted to listen to.

He sat there, the envelope on the passenger seat for company.

He looked away, out the window. People walking past looked blurred, as if he'd been crying. He rubbed his eyes. They were dry.

To his left, a grassy patch with a handful of trees. He focused on a squirrel, watched it sprint across ten feet of open ground and up the trunk of a tree. It stopped a few feet up, clung there, turned its head and stared at him.

Valerie Anderson, he heard it say. *Nothing but a lonely old woman who's a little too fond of the bottle.*

Carlos thought hard as he stared back at the squirrel. Someone knew his business. That was bad enough. But someone knew his private life, too, and that made Carlos extremely uncomfortable.

***

When he pulled up in his driveway, Maggie was at the door, waiting for him, Sofía in her arms.

He turned off the engine, pinched the envelope between thumb and fingers, climbed out of the car.

Maggie sauntered over to him, her flip-flops clacking against the soles of her feet, kissed his cheek. "What's so bad you had to come home?" she said, quietly, her eyes too bright and more purple than blue.

He leaned in, saw that Sofía was asleep. He ran his thumb lightly over her scalp, stroked the fair downy hair she'd inherited from her mother. "In the garden," he said, leading the way round the side of the house, towards the back.

"Grass needs cut," Maggie said.

"So cut it," he said.

"I'm just saying," she said.

"Well, don't."

"What the fuck's wrong?"

"Don't swear at me."

"Jesus, Charlie." Her chin dimpled.

He sat down on the bench at the back of the house. "Go put this in the safe." He held out the money. The finances and the paperwork and all that, Maggie's job. He struggled with numbers. No, that wasn't true. He could do it all right, he just chose not to. It bored him, whereas Maggie seemed to get something out of it.

"What is it?" she said.

"Deposit."

"Nice," she said. "You better take Sofía, then."

Once Maggie'd gone, he turned Sofía to face the garden. Little stretches and a pop of her lips and her lips widened and she smiled and then it was gone. She was still asleep. "Shame your daddy's not much of a gardener," he whispered to her. "Mummy neither." Not many little girls in Edinburgh had their own garden.

Pity you rarely got the weather to take

advantage of it. Usually raining or windy or both. Today was dry and the wind hadn't come out to play yet.

One day, when she was older, they'd appreciate it together.

For now he'd sit here with her and she could sleep and he could enjoy his garden. He'd worked hard enough for it.

He closed his eyes after a bit, but the inside of his head was too busy. His eyes sprang open again.

"It's okay," he said when Maggie returned.

"What is?"

"The grass. Doesn't need cut. Not yet."

"Charlie," she said.

He said nothing.

"Carlos, look at me," she said.

He looked at her. He liked looking at her. She was pretty, didn't need make up. She was half his age, twice as smart. She'd gained a little weight having Sofía and it suited her. She was sexy even with baby sick on her sleeve.

She said, "Are you going to tell me what's going on?"

He took a breath through his nose, smelled her perfume, something delicate, rising above Sofía's sweet milky smell.

"Mum spoken to you recently?" he asked.

"Only once since I told her to sober up. She phoned. Wanted to know if you'd fix her tap."

He smiled. "That again. No mention of Sofía?"

"Yeah." Maggie glanced at her feet. "Said she was sorry."

"I don't doubt it."

"Neither do I. You don't think I'm wrong, do you?" Her tongue flicked out, licked her lips. "Is that what this is about?"

"How can you think that?" He shook his head.

"So why all the interest in your mother?"

"You won't believe this," he said. He didn't believe it himself. He took hold of Maggie's hand. "Someone wants her dead."

***

His mother answered the door, eyes red-rimmed like she hadn't been sleeping. She looked like she'd just thrown her clothes on. Her cardigan was buttoned up all wrong.

"*Madre*," he said. It annoyed her when he spoke Spanish.

She didn't let on, asked, "What are you doing here?"

"You still got that leaky tap?"

"The one in the bathroom?"

He shrugged.

"Well, yes," she said.

"Then I'll try to fix it."

"It's not the washer."

"Did I say it was?"

She shrugged.

He said, "I'll take a look anyway."

"Oh," she said. She straightened up, maybe realising he hadn't come here to chastise. "This is an unexpected surprise. What's brought it on?"

He looked away. "You phoned."

"That never worked before."

"Well, you've been going on about it long enough."

She peered at him down her long nose,

kinked in the middle where she'd broken it on a skiing holiday, along with her leg.

"You want the tap fixed?" he said. "Or should I go?"

She folded her thin arms, nibbled her pale lower lip. "You're not working today?"

"It's slow," he said. "Left Dan to take care of things."

"Maggie said he was on holiday."

Maggie hadn't mentioned that. "You spoke about Dan?"

"I asked how things were going at the salon."

"Well, Dan's back, as of this morning."

"Must have been a short trip."

"Yeah," he said. "Couple of nights. All he could afford on the salary I pay him."

She nodded, unfolded herself, tucked her lip away. "Come on in."

**

The sitting room was a shrine to seventies bad taste. Bucket seats, white leather couch, brown and orange shag carpet and stripey psychedelic wallpaper. Reminders of her prime, no doubt.

She said, "You want coffee before you start?"

"*Si,*" he said. Before he started what? The décor was fucking with his head, making him dizzy. Oh, yeah, fixing a leaking tap. Which he had no intention of doing. He wouldn't know where to begin.

He moved a magazine off the settee. It squeaked when he flopped down into it. Placed the magazine on top of the glass coffee table, next to the old-fashioned dial-operated red telephone, one of those models that once upon a time everybody used to have.

"You don't have any tools," she said.

"Thought I could use George's."

"I imagined you'd bring your own."

"I don't have any. I'm not a plumber."

"Right."

"You still have them?"

"You have to ask?" She disappeared into the kitchen. She shouted, "How's Maggie?"

"Good," he said.

"What? Speak up."

"Good," he said, louder.

"And Sofía?"

"Good."

"How's Sofía?"

"Great," he said, louder.

"You know, I'm so sorry, but I'm just grateful she landed on the cushion. No harm done. And whatever Maggie thinks, the drink has nothing to do with it, it's just me, you know me, clumsy…"

She babbled on. She'd never liked Maggie. The fact that Maggie was twenty years younger than Carlos had a lot to do with it. And Maggie had never warmed to her as a result. After what had happened with Sofía, the temperature of their relationship had grown decidedly cool. He tuned his mother out. Picked up the magazine, flicked through it. Gardening magazine. His mother didn't have a garden. Well, she shared a garden with the other members of the tenement, but there was a lawn, and that was all. No reason that she should have a gardening magazine. Maybe she was thinking of coming round to his, giving it a make-over.

She could leave his fucking garden alone.

God, she knew how to make him angry.

When she returned with the coffee — milk jug and sugar bowl on a tray, despite the fact that neither of them took sugar, and a selection of biscuits which he knew neither of them would touch – he asked her about the magazine. "You renting an allotment or something?"

"Not mine," she said, her cheeks turning pink.

"Whose, then?" he said.

She pressed the plunger on the cafetiere. Her hand was shaking. "Just a friend."

Just a friend. She'd had a few of those since George died. "A good friend?" he asked.

"Well," she said. She poured a cup of coffee for him, half a cup for herself. "Well, yes, I'd have said so at one point. But now I'd have to say no."

"Sorry to hear that," Carlos said. "You want to talk about it?"

"I doubt any good would come of that." She reached behind her, pulled a bottle of vodka from the side of the settee. "Don't say a word." She unscrewed the top. "This is my house. My vodka. I can do as I wish."

He said nothing, picked up his cup, drank his coffee. She made good coffee. Hadn't always been that way. When he was a kid her coffee tasted like crap. He remembered his dad drinking *cortados*. Coffee the way it should be drunk. But back then Carlos's palate was too immature to appreciate it. And by the time he was old enough to do so, Pablo Morales had disappeared from their lives.

"So," she said, pouring a generous amount of vodka into her cup. "Work's slow?" She screwed the top back on the bottle.

"Yeah," he said, but he could have said anything. She'd already decided what she was going to say next.

She took a sip of her drink, blinked slowly. "Plumbing," she said. "It's never too late."

"*Cago en tu leche.*"

She frowned, pouted her lips. "Something about milk?"

Something about shitting in it, but he wasn't about to tell her that. "I'm very fucking sorry I never became a plumber, Mama."

That's right. Now she'd snapped to attention. He'd never match up to the late George Anderson, his mother's second husband, plumber fucking extraordinaire. Carlos changed the subject. Last thing he needed right now was more anger he didn't have an outlet for.

Things were about to get complicated.

"Mum," he said. "This may seem like a strange question, but you haven't annoyed anybody recently, have you?"

She grinned, lips quivering, exposing dull yellow teeth. "Me? Always annoying people."

"But annoyed somebody very badly."

"I usually annoy people very well. Ask Maggie."

"You know what I mean."

"What a strange question." Her eyes shone, twin beams of pencil torches. He watched her eyelids come down, the left slightly quicker than the right. Then they rose again. "I really have no idea what you mean."

The tanning salon was a front. Carlos had bought it many years ago from Florida Al, a fat Geordie who liked to wear Hawaiian shirts.

Carlos wasn't sure why the fat lad wasn't called Hawaiian Al, but nicknames don't always make sense. Al had been using the salon as a base for a gun-running operation. All Carlos did, he just took his concept up a league. Gave it the balls that fat *verga* never had.

Carlos didn't kill people. He made the arrangements for someone else to do the killing. He was a broker, a go-between, an intermediary, an agent. At various times, he'd called himself by all these names.

But he wasn't a killer.

Plenty of people knew how to contact him directly. Receiving the package hadn't been that much of a surprise. The fact that someone knew that Valerie Anderson was Carlos Morales's mother worried him. He was careful to hide that, never spoke to anyone about his private life. But what was deeply troubling was the fact that the letter had arrived addressed to Charlie. There were only two people who called him Charlie: Maggie, and his mother.

He'd discussed the situation with Maggie and they'd agreed he had no choice. He had to ask his mum straight out. "*Mamá*," he said. "Why would someone want you dead?"

She shuffled in her seat. "Why what?"

"You heard me."

She picked up her cup, took a large sip. "What nonsense is this? It's not funny."

"I'm perfectly serious."

"Why would you think someone wants me dead?" she said.

He couldn't answer that. Not now.

***

When he got home, Maggie was alone in the sitting room watching TV. Carlos noticed she'd been biting her fingernails.

"How did it go?" she said.

"Where's Sofía?"

"Sleeping. How did it go?" she repeated.

He told her what had happened.

Maggie shook her head. "You have to tell her."

"Tell her what?"

"The truth. About you. About the business."

"I can't do that." His mother had no idea what he really did for a living and Carlos wanted to keep it that way.

"Then what? This is eating you up, Charlie."

Was it? He hadn't noticed. She was probably right. He was trying not to notice, but he did want to find out who'd paid for the contract. It wasn't just curiosity either. His mother could be a pain in the arse, sure, but he couldn't believe someone would hate her enough to want her dead. And at a very decent price, too.

"What are you going to do?" Maggie asked.

"I'm going to look in on Sofía," he said, watching Maggie tighten her lips, shake her head fast, like she was trying to dislodge water from her ears. A familiar gesture that had become more exaggerated since Sofía was born.

"And then what?" Maggie said.

"One step at a time, *mi esposa impaciente*. Patience, love."

***

Back at his mother's a few days later, sitting on the settee with another cup of coffee. She sat forward in one of the bucket seats to refill her glass from the bottle of vodka on the coffee table.

"I've been worried," she said. "You got me flustered, all your talk of people wanting me dead. I haven't slept."

"I'm sorry," he said. She looked tired. But then she'd looked tired for years.

"Thanks. But that hardly helps."

"I know." He shifted in his seat, leaned closer. "I need to tell you something."

She glanced away. Took a sip. "Why do I feel like I don't want to hear this?"

He could leave now. He could walk away. Everything could stay as it had always been.

Instead, he told her everything. It was the only way he could be sure.

She listened in silence.

When he'd finished, she said, "I don't believe a word of it."

He nodded. "I don't blame you."

"You've been doing this for years?"

"Long time, *si*."

"How could I not have known?"

"I'm careful."

"But still. You'd think a mother would know that her son was a... a monster." Her face was even paler than usual, her lips like hungry worms. "I should call the police."

"I can understand how you feel," he said. "But there would be no point. I'd just deny it. You'd sound like a crazy old drunk."

"You think that's what I am?" She placed her glass on the table, carefully. It made only the tiniest sound. "What about you? What happened to your sanity? What happened to your conscience, for God's sake?"

"Please, Mum. I can do without the moralising. I don't mention your drinking, do I?"

Her eyes widened. "You just *did*. Anyway, there's a bit of a bloody difference between... killing people and enjoying a drink."

"Maybe," he said. "Although I don't think Maggie sees it that way."

She wiped a drip off her glass with her forefinger. "She knew what you did when she married you?" She licked her finger, wiped it against her thumb.

"Oh, yeah. Sometimes I think that was the

reason."

"Yet she hates me drinking?"

"Never mind Maggie, Mum."

"How can I not mind? She won't let me see my own granddaughter."

"I know."

"She's never liked me."

"I know. But just try to focus. Tell me if you can think of anyone who'd want you out of the way."

"Out of the way." She closed her eyes. "Jesus," she said. "Why should I give a hoot about helping you? Not as if you're helping me."

"You could help yourself by not drinking."

"Listen to yourself."

"You're missing the point."

"You may think so."

"Mum, shut up."

"What did you say?"

"You heard."

She shut up.

"Somebody wants you dead," Carlos said. "Enough to pay me a substantial sum of money to make that happen. You can get all moral on me after we've figured out who it is. Unless you don't care."

She stared into space, said nothing.

"Well," he said. "Do you?"

"Of course I do." She picked up her glass again. "Of course I want to know who hates me that much."

"That's what I thought."

She gulped down the rest of her drink. "So how do we find that out?"

***

Carlos took the long way home, listened to some *flamenco* for a few minutes, but it was too tortured and mournful for his mood. He stuck on one of Maggie's compilation CDs instead. Good driving music. Nice tempo but relaxing too.

And Carlos needed to relax. Seeing his mother at the best of times was a strain. Tonight, well, he'd felt the back of his eyeballs start to hurt and that was always a bad sign.

His mother's reaction had seemed genuine. What he'd told her had surprised and shocked her. Either that or he didn't know her like he thought he did. No, there was no act there. And even if he was wrong, if she had known, there was no reason for her to want to have herself killed. Made no sense. He'd heard of it before, of course. People who were depressed enough to want to commit suicide, but couldn't actually do it, sometimes they'd hire a hit man to do it for them. Fools. If you can't kill yourself, there's a good reason. Means you don't want to fucking die. But even though his mum was a functioning alcoholic, she wasn't that depressed. Fair enough, she wasn't happy about not getting to see Sofía, but Carlos doubted she believed Maggie would stay angry with her for long.

Which pointed the finger of suspicion at Maggie. Yeah, it was crazy and he didn't want to consider it, but he had no choice. The facts were that Maggie knew who his mother was; she knew what Carlos did for a living; she had easy access to ten grand in cash; and she called him Charlie. But why would she want his mother dead? Because of what happened with Sofía? Made no sense either.

He turned up the volume, started to sing

along with the music.

The answer would come to him. It always did.

**

Maggie said, "You're sure?"

"She practically admitted it," Carlos said. "Kept saying she was no good to anybody. Just an old drunk who'd be better off dead." It felt natural to lie to his wife. He wasn't sure why he'd never done it before.

"She said that?" Maggie turned off the TV. "Wow. I mean, fucking wow." She put her hand to her head, grabbed a handful of hair, combed it through her fingers. "I can't believe it."

"I know. It's fucked up."

"Wow." The skin around her eyes creased. "It's insane."

"That's my mother."

Maggie shook her head. "Wonder how she found out."

"No idea."

"Maybe it's a test." She bit her lip, let it go. "Maybe she doesn't really want to be…

expurgated."

Carlos looked at her, waiting for her to say more.

"Maybe she found out what you do and she just wants to see how far you'll go."

Carlos nodded slowly, remembering the word his mother had used. "See how much of a monster her son is? Could be."

Maggie sat down, crossed one ankle over the other. "So what are you going to do?"

"What she wants."

"You mean...?"

"*Si*. I'm going to kill the old bitch."

"Holy shit," Maggie said. "You can't do that."

"If she's had enough, I'll be putting her out of her misery. And if she's playing a game, I'm going to make sure I win."

"Even if it means killing her?"

"It's what she wants."

"She can't want that."

"Well, it's what she's paid me for. Wouldn't want to disappoint her, would I? I'm a professional, after all."

"Fuck, Charlie." Maggie rubbed the palm of

her hand on her thigh. "You're serious."

"I didn't ask for this. And I didn't decide on the stakes."

"Still..."

"'Still' what? I thought you didn't like her? Didn't want her round Sofía?"

"Yeah, but that doesn't mean I'd want her... done."

"Done?"

"You know... expurgated."

"She won't be expurgated. Only Richie can do that."

"You know what I mean. Richie, Jordan, same thing."

Carlos nodded. "I'd rather not use Jordan either."

"I thought you and him had an understanding."

He shrugged. "This is personal. It's more than just a business transaction. Something I need to do myself."

"Shit," she said. She laughed. "Sorry. I'm just... trying to let this sink in."

"There's more," he said, and waited for her

to calm herself. "I'll need some help. Someone I can trust."

"Hardly spoilt for choice, then."

"No," he said. "What are you doing next week? Tuesday night, maybe?"

"Me?" She widened her eyes as what he was asking her sunk in. "Charlie, I couldn't."

"You could. Easy. I'll do the hard part. You don't need to see that. I just need you to give me a hand afterwards."

"A hand? What does that mean?"

"Getting rid of the body."

"I really don't think —"

"I'll make sure it's wrapped up, all sanitised and that. Promise. Just keep an eye out for me while I get the body out of her flat and downstairs. Help me get it into the car. Not ours, I'll steal one. We drive to the Forth, lose the body. After that, we'll dump the car and head home. I'll maybe need some help getting the body onto my shoulders, but I can carry it from there. Other than that, you won't need to touch it."

"Just warn you if somebody's around?"

"That's it. You'd be a lookout."

She lowered her gaze. After a bit she looked at him again and said, "You're going through with this." Not a question.

He nodded.

"Then steal a van," she said.

Jesus fucking Christ. She was going along with it. He stayed perfectly calm. "You think?"

"Easier to get the body in and out."

"Yeah," he said, nodding. He clenched his fists. "Yeah. You thinking a Transit?"

"Doesn't need to be that big. Didn't Jordan's old man have three bodies in the back of his?"

"That wasn't his van."

She shook her head, exasperated. "But there were three bodies in it, right?"

"Yeah."

"So nick one of those vans, whatever it was. It'll be plenty big enough."

His fingernails were digging into the palms of his hands. "I'll ask Jordan."

"I know a good car thief if you need one. Brother of Arlene's boyfriend."

"Your sister can certainly pick them."

"You can fucking talk."

"He's reliable?"

"He nicks cars to order."

Carlos unclenched his fists, locked his trembling fingers together. "Kids've got too much money these days."

"And we should take a leaf out of their book. Burn the van afterwards."

"Get rid of any evidence? Not a bad idea." He waited, throat dry. "So we're on?"

"I don't know. I don't know, Charlie. This is a step beyond."

"For me too. But it's going to happen, Maggie. With or without your help. I'd like it to be the former."

Say no, Maggie.

"Let me think about it," she said.

2

When Carlos arrived at his mother's flat, she was drinking coffee and Jordan was sitting opposite on the settee with the dregs of a glass of milk on the table in front of him.

"Everything okay?" Carlos said.

"We've been having a lovely chat," his mother said.

Carlos wasn't sure for a second, then saw her lips curl slightly and decided she was being sarcastic. Jordan wasn't exactly chatty at the best of times. Not surprising given what the poor kid had gone through. Course, this whole situation was complex, what with Jordan and Richie's families having pretty much annihilated one another about eighteen months ago.

Luckily, with Richie still in prison and likely to stay there for a long, long time, that wasn't a problem.

Carlos didn't feel too bad about it, though. He'd needed someone to replace Richie. And Jordan visited Richie's mother regularly, even now, which was something. Just sat there, neither of them speaking, holding hands. He'd seen them there that first time at the Home. Jordan was a blank. And Richie's mother, Liz, hadn't spoken in years.

It was Richie's fault that Carlos and Jordan had met. Richie'd asked Carlos to check in on Liz, see how she was coping. Carlos couldn't see the point, wasn't intending hanging around, just dropping off some fresh flowers and scarpering, but when he got there he'd found this kid with her, a boy, barely a teenager, and remembered seeing the picture of them together in the newspaper. Part of the media frenzy. Kid Rescues Brain-Damaged Woman From Inferno. Not to mention the horror show inside the country cottage as body after body was discovered. Fascinating. Then all the speculation. Nobody knew who'd killed who. It was all guesswork. The fire saw to that.

And of the only two survivors, Liz couldn't speak and the kid wouldn't speak. Too traumatised, apparently.

And he wasn't the only one. Richie couldn't handle it. Went berserk in the slammer, killed a guard, which meant that he'd probably never get out now. Anyway, no chance he'd get to visit his mum. Which is why he'd asked Carlos to go see her, and how Carlos had bumped into Jordan.

Carlos had spotted it right away. He'd seen it in the photos. He saw it the minute he saw Jordan in the flesh. The kid was dead behind the eyes. Just like Richie used to be.

"Nice of you to visit," Carlos had said to Jordan. "But why?"

Jordan shrugged.

Carlos cleared his throat, lowered his voice. "You can tell me."

No response.

Carlos said, "Tell me what you did."

Jordan looked him in the eye.

"It can be our secret," Carlos said.

Are you a poof or something? Sounded like a young lad's voice, one on the point of breaking, flitting about like it wasn't sure which register suited best. Carlos hadn't seen Jordan open his mouth, but he was the only kid in the room. *Well?*

"No." Carlos smiled. "No, no." He waited a moment. "Is it because you feel guilty? Is that why you're here?"

I feel nothing.

"Good," Carlos said. "That's excellent. Anyway, I suppose the bitch got what she deserved."

Jordan looked at him again.

The bitch. Liz's daughter. Richie's sister.

"I thought so," Carlos said. "I know how you must feel."

Jordan stared at his feet, tapped the toes of his trainers on the floor.

"You sorry about what you did?" Carlos asked.

Why would I be sorry?

"You like money, Jordan?"

The kid shrugged again.

"You and me," Carlos said. "I think we'll get along just fine."

And they had done. The kid needed an outlet and spilled everything to Carlos eventually. Run out of bullets or he'd still be there pumping slugs into her, he'd said. Or at least that's what Carlos heard him say. Something had happened with Jordan's dad, too, but he wouldn't elaborate. He claimed he didn't feel anything, but there was something there, something raw that Carlos knew was best avoided.

Jordan was good. Professional. Ruthless. Problem was he could only do local jobs. He lived with his grandmother and she kept tabs on him, protective of him now that her sons were dead. Carlos didn't know what had happened to Jordan's mother, but she was out of the picture. So, while Jordan could sneak out for the night easily enough, he couldn't pop down to London for a couple of days. But that was okay. Carlos had wound down the operation anyway and just the occasional job now and again was fine with him. Once Jordan got a bit older, maybe they'd pick up again.

Anyway, it would appear from tonight's showing that Jordan hadn't said anything to Carlos's mother. Maggie didn't care for him much, found the silences hard to bear, although she'd only ever met him a couple of times to deliver his money to him and claimed that he said, "Clever," when she took the money out of the pram the first time, and "Thanks" the second time. But she conceded that he was good at what he did. Carlos had expected his mother would get herself plastered as usual tonight, give them a piece of her booze-addled mind, but she looked as sober as he'd seen her in ages.

Carlos tossed the bodybag onto the shag carpet. "Hope you like the colour," he said.

"You sure you want to go through with this?" his mum asked.

"It's the only way."

He didn't want to discuss this again. They'd been over it enough times already. They really needed to get moving now. Maggie was waiting outside in the Ford Escort van her sister's boyfriend had nicked to order, trying to keep herself relaxed by listening to her iPod, and

Carlos was due to give her a bell once he was done. He promised her it'd be quick. She'd be ringing him to see what the problem was if he didn't hurry.

He didn't hurry. He sat down next to Jordan, shifting the gun tucked down the back of his waistband as it dug into his spine.

She *had* to ring. She had to tell him to stop what he was about to do. This was her last chance.

"Maybe it wasn't her," his mother said.

"Doesn't matter," he said. Maybe Maggie'd taken out the contract, maybe not. But either way, she should make him stop this craziness. He was about to kill his mother, for Christ's sake. Her silence made her guilty of something unforgivable, even if he couldn't pinpoint it just yet. "Whatever way you look at it, if she doesn't put a stop to this, she's a bitch from hell." And she'd signed her own death warrant.

"I'll give her ten more minutes," he said to his mother. "And then…"

"I'm dead," she said, nodding. "Thanks, Maggie."

They sat in silence, Carlos counting down the minutes, then the seconds, and finally, he said, "If you were looking for a monster, I think you've found one." He took the gun out of his waistband and handed it to Jordan. "You'll be needing this," he said. "It's not pretty but it'll do the job."

***

Maggie arrived a minute after he'd texted her. He answered the door, aware of a dull throb behind his eyes when he looked at her.

"Is it done?" she asked.

He turned away from her, led her into the sitting room, pointed at the bodybag, filled out, zipped up.

"Shit," she said. "You did it."

"Of course I did it."

"Shit," she said again. "Do you feel okay?"

"Fine."

"Really?"

"Yeah. How should I feel?"

"I dunno. In pain. Emotional. Horrible."

"I'm fine," Carlos said.

They stood for a minute, looking at each other, at the bodybag, back at each other. "So," Carlos said. "Give me a hand to lift this?"

Maggie didn't move.

"What?"

"How can you be 'fine'?" she asked.

"How many times do I need to say it?"

"I just find it hard to believe—"

"Maggie, we don't have time for this. Help me get the bag onto my shoulder."

"You can't be 'fine'."

"I assure you, I'm just fine. *Por favor*." He indicated the bag.

"You're right." She stepped forward. "You're right," she said again. "Looks heavy. You going to manage it?"

"No problem. Diet of vodka, she weighs next to nothing."

"Dead weight though." She looked at him, realised what she'd said. She laughed. "I'm sorry," she said.

"What for?"

"It's not funny."

"No," he said. "It isn't."

"I'm just nervous. I can't get my head round this."

"Don't think," he said. "Act."

"I didn't think you'd go through with it."

"Don't think," he said, louder.

"I should have stopped you."

They stared at the bag. He'd thought all bodybags were black. But the mortuary only had a spare one in tan.

"Charlie," she said.

"Yeah?"

"You killed your mother."

He grabbed her wrist. "For Christ's sake, Maggie. You knew I was going to do it. Why are you acting so surprised?"

"I didn't…" She pulled her arm away.

"You didn't what?"

"Forget it. It's done." She rubbed her wrist.

He spoke quietly. "You wish it wasn't? Maybe you should have talked me out of it."

"Not my call."

He took a long breath through his nose. Smelled Maggie's face cream. She was wearing lipstick too. For her, this was just a night out.

"Fair enough," he said. "Are you going to stand there, or are you going to help?"

***

Once Carlos had watched a delivery guy carry a washing machine on his back up three flights of stairs. Impressive. Even more impressive, the same guy had taken the old one away with him on the way back down. In comparison, carrying a body down a single flight of stairs shouldn't be too much of a task. Carlos took a couple of steps towards the door, testing out the weight on his shoulders.

Maggie looked at him.

"It's not so bad," he said.

***

He was wrong. He'd only managed three steps and already his legs felt leaden. And he kept thinking he was going to topple forwards. He couldn't balance properly, wanted to put his hand on the rail but knew if he did that the body would slip. Maybe the bodybag hadn't been such a great idea after all. This was an extra heavy duty job. Greater 'leakage protection', he was told, after he'd complained about the colour. Sounded just fine as a sales pitch, but the reality was that the bag weighed more than the standard model.

He considered turning round, walking backwards. Felt like it'd be a damn sight easier, leaning against the slope. But he needed to see where he was going. He'd stumble, fall, land on his neck or something.

Mierda. At this pace, he'd be here all night. Somebody might come home. Always a risk, even though it was late. If they did, there was the wedge under the front door and Maggie poised to stall them. But if someone who was already at home decided to head on out for some reason, there wasn't much he could do. Couldn't hide. Couldn't run away. He'd just have to own up. Which would ruin everything.

The thought had occurred to him before. He tried to remember why he'd decided it wouldn't be a problem.

Ideally, his mother's murder should have

been committed elsewhere. But this was all for Maggie's benefit. Not that she could appreciate it. Or would if she could. He'd just have to get on with it. Tuesday night. One in the morning. Nobody was going to be coming in or out. Fuck it, everything'd be fine.

***

He limped his way down the rest of the steps, one careful step after another. By the time he reached the bottom, sweat was running into his eyes and the muscles in his neck and shoulder felt like they were being twisted around each other and pulled so tight they were about to snap. His thighs burned.

But so far, so good. Only ten feet between him and the front door. He took a breath, staggered forwards.

A few steps later, Maggie bent down, removed the wooden wedge from under the door. She fumbled the wedge, sprang back when it bounced on the floor with a clack. "Shit," she said. "Shit, shit." She picked up the wedge, her hand shaking. "Should I check outside?"

He wanted to nod but couldn't. And he was too out of breath to say anything. He let his eyes do the talking.

Yes.

She disappeared, returned a few seconds later. "Clear," she said. "I'll go open the van."

He still couldn't believe she was doing this.

***

Ten minutes later, Maggie removed her headphones, turned off her iPod. "Classical music. Bach," she said. "Thought I'd give it a go. Supposed to help you relax."

"And I thought you just didn't want to talk to me." Carlos grinned to show he wasn't serious.

"Hope Sofía's okay."

Their babysitter was a seventeen-year-old whose name Carlos couldn't remember. They'd used her before. Maggie was friends with her sister. Or someone. "She'll be just fine," he said. "Why don't you phone and check?"

"It's late," Maggie said. "I'm fretting. I have to worry about her, you know. Mother's duty."

He watched the white lines in the middle of the road, pushed the wheel of his palm against the steering wheel.

Maggie asked, "How's the shoulder?"

The pain was a fading ache now. "Gone," he said.

"Gone," Maggie said.

"Yeah," he said. "Just about."

Those white lines reminded him of when he was a kid, first time in a plane, looking out the window as they were about to land, still trying to work out how something so heavy could float in the air.

"What?" Maggie said.

"Nothing. Why?"

"You look like you're somewhere else."

"I do?" God, it was weird, but he felt some kind of sense of loss. Maybe it was because of what was going to happen to Maggie. A state of pre-mourning or something. His stomach felt empty. Not that he was hungry. It just felt like he hadn't eaten. And the sound of the car engine was too loud, high-pitched. Like an airplane.

"You know how I hate airports," he said, for something to say.

"I've noticed, yeah."

"You know why?"

She shrugged. "They're no fun. Nobody likes them. Security checks, all that crap."

"I've always hated them, long before the days of liquid bombs. First flight, I was nine or ten. We'd just got back from Spain, looking for Dad. The passengers were all clustered round the carousel at the baggage retrieval and there was this hubbub of chat floating around. You ever noticed airport acoustics?" He didn't wait for an answer. He was talking to himself anyway. "There's this swell of noise. You can pick out layers, but no words. And over the top you can hear the sound of rattling cutlery, like it's in your headphones, and someone's telling you he's dead. *Your father's dead*. And you look over to a coffee shop that's a hundred feet away and someone's stacking cups, that's all, and you go, fuck me, that's what I'm hearing, my dad's okay. That's what happened to me, anyway. After our failed trip to find Dad. But I thought my hearing was buggered for good, and it filled me with, I don't know, dread, I suppose, hearing that voice, and I felt this pressure behind my eyes and I burst into tears."

He felt her hand on his thigh, warming his tingling muscles.

"In fact, I wasn't so far wrong. My left ear's not so good, and maybe that's part of the problem. You know that, but did you know that my left eye's weaker than my right?"

"I didn't," she said. "But thanks for telling me."

"And my left foot's smaller than my right. My dad used to say that I was 'all right'. Funny guy, my dad. That was his best English joke. He was proud of it." He didn't want to tell her any more but he couldn't stop. "Ironic, my issues with airports. Cause up to that point, I believed I wanted to travel the world when I grew up. Used to have a model plane I took everywhere with me. A spitfire. War plane. Type 356-Mk 22. Teardrop canopy. Built it from a kit. Painted it camouflage colours. Green, light and dark brown. But the nose, for some reason, I painted the nose a dark blue. The underbelly was a pale cream. Apart from the decals on the wingtips, the eyes. They were blue, like the nose, and I spent a long time with a fine brush giving them perfect little evenly spaced eyelashes."

"Charlie."

"My mum bought me the plane. She worked for a travel agency. Spent her days selling holidays to places she never saw herself. I'd never flown before. I don't remember her flying either. Just that once. My dad left us nothing. Just disappeared without even saying goodbye. She married that rich fuck, George, who was able to take her places she'd only dreamed about. But that was a long time later. My dad, Pablo, he just walked away one day without so much as a goodbye kiss."

"Charlie."

"As a kid, that plane represented an escape route. And yeah, those guns fitted in the wings were probably significant, too."

"Charlie." She put her hand on his shoulder.

"Am I a monster?" he asked her.

She squeezed, fingers massaging the muscle. "Maybe in some people's eyes," she said.

"In my mother's, you mean."

She turned her head slightly, glanced through the loose chickenwire partition into the back. "Yes."

Carlos checked the rearview. Too dark to see much. But his brain compensated for the limitations of his eyes and he made out the bodybag, the heavy chains, the petrol cans, the holdall. "And in yours?"

She didn't reply.

"Well?"

"I'm here, ain't I?" she said.

"You are," he said. "I'm sorry about that."

She gave a little laugh. "It's okay."

But that wasn't what he'd meant.

"Tell me about you," he said.

"What do you mean?"

He wanted to know everything. There were plenty of things she hadn't told him. Not just the reason she'd taken out the contract on his mother. No, other things. Trivial things. Things he shouldn't care about but which seemed to matter now. He didn't know if there'd been a sandpit at her infant school; didn't know the name of the boy she first held hands with; didn't know if she could ride a horse; didn't know the name of her favourite dolls or teddy bears; didn't know her mother's maiden name.

Sentimentality. He had to put a stop to it. Think of something else.

He pictured them dragging the bodybag out of the van, laying it on the ground. He heard himself tell Maggie he wanted to say goodbye. Saw himself pull down the zipper. Jordan's face staring back at him. "Come closer," Carlos said to Maggie. "Say a few words." She kept her distance, a few feet away, said she'd rather not. He nodded, said he understood. He pulled the zipper all the way down. He said, "Okay," to Jordan and the kid sat up, hair matted to his forehead from the heat inside the bodybag, gun in his hand. And Carlos said to Maggie, "Are you sure there isn't anything you'd like to say?"

If she still didn't confess, facing certain death like that, then Carlos could assume it wasn't her who'd arranged the contract. And maybe he could let her go, like he'd promised his mother. Jordan, they'd agreed, was just to scare Maggie into admitting her guilt. Whatever happened afterwards, they'd have to divorce. He'd make sure he got custody. That wouldn't be a problem.

Course, the reality was that Carlos couldn't think of a scenario that didn't end up with Maggie having to take a long nap in the body-bag.

That's what he meant. It made his heart twitch.

But for now, all he said was, "Nothing. It doesn't matter."

***

A few minutes later, they were driving along a country road and Carlos was remembering his first time with Maggie – how she'd led him into his bedroom, yanked his trousers down to his knees, buried her head in his crotch, and moaned as she sucked and moaned and took her head away briefly to say *fuck fuck fuck yeah* and sucked and moaned until he spasmed and shuddered like a man in an electric chair, and then after she cleaned up with her t-shirt, she steered his mouth from nipple to nipple to bellybutton to crotch, telling him what he should do and where and how hard and fast and deep until she came in a series of *fuck fuck fuck yeahs*, but he just couldn't get it up again no matter how she coaxed and teased, so they didn't fuck until the following weekend — when he saw a flashing light in the rearview.

Couldn't be. Not now.

"*Mierda*," he said.

"What?" Maggie asked.

"Behind us."

She looked over her shoulder. "Shit. So much for my idea of taking the back roads."

"Just our fucking luck. You'd think the cops would have something better to do with their time than haul us up at two in the morning." He couldn't think of a way out of this.

"We'll have to pull over," Maggie said, confirming that she was out of ideas too.

"With a corpse in the back?"

"What do you suggest? This piece of junk can't outrun a police car."

She was right. They didn't have a choice. He slowed to a crawl.

***

The police car overtook them, pulled into the side of the road, and stopped.

Carlos swore. He kept swearing. *Puta, puta, puta.* Fuck.

After a bit, somebody climbed out of the car. A young guy. Late teens, maybe. He wasn't in uniform.

"He's not a cop," Carlos said to Maggie.

"Maybe he's a detective."

"Too young."

"Whoever he is, he's got a gun."

So he did. And he was pointing it their way. But it was okay.

"Don't worry," Carlos said. "That's a Glock. Almost definitely a replica." Cause even Carlos, with all his connections, found it almost impossible to buy a reasonably priced fully operational Glock these days. He owned one once, but Richie's crazy dad had stolen it just before he got himself killed. Carlos didn't know

55

for sure, but he suspected it was the same gun Jordan had used that night at the cottage. Unlike tonight, where he'd had to give Jordan a converted Valtro 98 "gas alarm" pistol. Lot of them about at the moment. Good business in buying replicas in bulk in Berlin, smuggling them into the UK, and adapting them to fire live rounds. So Carlos was told. But Glocks? Apparently they were hard to come by, priced accordingly. Supply and demand. But there were shitloads of replicas sold before the ban was introduced in October last year. So either this cop-teenager had more money than was likely, or that was a replica in his hand. Carlos was betting on the latter.

What the fucker was doing out here in a police car pretending to be a cop with a Glock, Carlos had no idea. He smiled, wound down the window, stuck his head out. Felt good to get some cool air on his skin. The night smelt of fox piss and rapeseed. "*Problemo*, Officer?"

The guy said nothing. Got closer to the car. "Turn off the engine and get out."

"Why?"

He waved the gun in Maggie's direction. His hand was big, fingers thick, looked swollen. "Tell him."

That was interesting. Almost as if he knew her.

And Maggie, well, she didn't look scared at all. She leaned across and turned off the engine.

"You a joyrider?" Carlos asked him. Seemed like a logical guess.

"Get out."

"Do what he says, Carlos," Maggie said.

"You heard her."

"I don't think so," Carlos said.

"Get the fuck out."

"I don't the fuck think so."

"If you don't, I'll kill you." He looked at Carlos, didn't move. "I'll shoot you in the head."

Carlos stared at him, pretty sure he was right about the Glock being a replica. Pretty damn fucking sure. Yeah. "Go on, then," Carlos said.

"Eh?"

"Kill me."

The guy's lips tightened. He said, "I want

you to get out first."

"I know."

"You better do it," Maggie said.

"Listen to her."

Carlos said, "I'm fine where I am."

"You have to do what you're told."

"*No posible.* Sorry." He didn't know what was going on here, but he was going to find out. "Why don't you tell me what you want?"

The guy looked at Maggie, then back at Carlos. "I want you out of the van, standing the fuck right here."

"Is it the van you want?" Carlos asked. "Or me? Or my wife?"

"I told you." He was getting twitchy, jerking the gun around. "Just get the fuck out."

"Listen," Carlos said. "How about you fuck off back to your police car and drive away. Then we can all get on with what we were doing."

"Right. I'm going to shoot you."

Carlos folded his arms. "And I'm going to sit right here."

"You can't do that."

"Why not?"

"Cause I'll…"

"Shoot me?"

"Yeah."

"Glad that's settled."

The guy blinked hard. "You think I'm fucking messing around?"

Carlos uncrossed his arms. "How did you get the car?"

"Huh?"

"Stealing a cop car can't be easy."

He said, "What's it to you?"

"Just saying," Carlos said. "Must have taken a bit of planning. A bit of know-how."

"Not really. Just hung around Lothian Road. Only a matter of time before a police car showed up."

"Hmm," Carlos said. "I bet they didn't leave the door open and the key in the ignition."

"Got a technique," he said. "See —" He broke off as the passenger door clicked open.

Carlos turned to see Maggie getting out of the car. "Wait," he said.

"It's okay," she said, the door snicking shut behind her.

He watched her walk round the front of the van, no hesitation, sidle up to the joyrider.

"A police car," she said to him. "I didn't expect that."

"I'm good."

"So I see." She fingered her hair. "My husband doesn't think your gun's loaded, you know."

"Doesn't he?" He looked at Carlos. "You don't?"

"Maggie," Carlos said. "Don't taunt him."

"He thinks I'm taunting you," Maggie said to the joyrider. "Do you think so?"

"What I think," the guy said. "I think I should blow this fucker away."

"What's your problem?" Carlos asked. "You got some issue with me, spit it out? I'm getting bored of this."

"Bored? You're getting fucking bored?" The guy twisted his body, pointed the gun at the police car and fired. The windscreen exploded.

"*Mierda.*" Carlos felt the explosion reverberate in his bowels, the sound of the windscreen shattering like an after-effect in his veins. He glanced in the rearview, saw the body-

60

bag wriggle. Thank Christ. They'd left the zipper undone just enough to allow air into the bag. Should mean Jordan would be able to get the bag open from the inside. Wasn't the plan, of course. But the plan was all gone to fuck. From now on, there was no fucking plan.

The joyrider said, "If you don't get out of there right now, I'll shoot you where you sit. Last chance."

Looked like everybody was on their last chance tonight.

"What does it matter?" Carlos asked.

"I don't want Maggie having to drive with your blood all over the place."

Maggie?

The joyrider knew where to find them, he knew Maggie's name. This was definitely no accidental encounter.

"Maggie?" Carlos said, looking at his wife.

She nestled in close to the joyrider, stood facing Carlos. "You killed your mother," she said. "You crossed a line, Charlie. How do I know that you won't kill me? Or Sofía?"

Holy shit. Maggie was behind this? Bad

enough that she'd want to get rid of his mum, but she was planning on getting rid of him as well? Fuck, what a bitch. Carlos felt stupid to have been so misled for so long.

"Christ's sake," he said. "Don't be fucking ridiculous."

"Is it?" Maggie said. "I thought long and hard about it. If you can bump off your mother, nobody's safe. Seems fucking logical to me."

"I'd never hurt Sofía."

"Right," Maggie said. "But you'd hurt me?"

"I didn't say that."

"You don't know how scary you are, Charlie. What you do. And it's bad enough when I'm not involved. But look what you've made me do now. I'm an accessory to murder. You think I like driving around with that thing in the back?" Her chin wobbled. "It fucking creeps me out. You creep me out. I need to protect myself."

He could tell her the truth. But, he thought, it was too late for that.

He reached forward and turned the engine on.

"Hey," the guy said. "What d'you think you're

doing? You're not going anywhere."

No, but the engine was making enough noise to allow Jordan to get the zip pulled down without being heard.

"I'm cold all of a sudden," Carlos said. "Just wanted to warm my hands."

"Turn it off."

"Just a couple of minutes."

"Turn it off!"

Carlos sighed, turned it off. Jordan was out of the bag now, but Carlos needed to keep talking, make a noise so Jordan could get out of the van. "Do you have a name?" he asked.

"Why do you want to know?"

"Don't you think I deserve to know the name of the man who kills me?"

"Should I tell him?" the guy asked Maggie.

"It's Bob," she said to Carlos.

"Bob," Carlos repeated.

"My sister's boyfriend."

Carlos tapped his fingertips together. It was tough not to look, see if the kid was out of the vehicle yet. But Carlos focused his attention on Bob. "You're the guy who got the van for us?"

"Yeah," he said.

"Gave Maggie all that info about burning it?"

"Yeah."

"So you're a killer as well as a car thief and arsonist?"

"Only once."

Carlos looked him in the eye. The bastard wasn't bluffing. "So what's between you and Maggie?" he asked. "Why would you kill me for her? What'd she offer you? Money? Sex?"

Bob was about to speak when there was a muscle-clenching bang and something slapped against the side of the van. Carlos made out a dark splotch above Bob's nose, and then Bob swayed, fell forward, bounced off the bonnet and slumped to the ground.

Maggie jumped back, and when she saw Jordan with his still-smoking gun pointed at her, she ran.

Carlos said, "No," as he shoved the door open and scooped up Bob's Glock off the road. "No, Jordan," he said. "Maggie, stop."

She looked behind her, still running, beyond

the police car.

Carlos aimed at her. "Maggie," he said.

She kept looking at him, stumbling side-ways.

His hand was steady. He squeezed the trigger.

A flash in his hand and her leg buckled under her. She fell into the grass at the side of the road. "Shit," she said, in a strangled voice. "You fucking bastard. This fucking hurts. Fuck, it hurts."

That's a bonus, Carlos thought, and slammed his fist into the van door.

***

She started to crawl forward. There was a barbed-wire fence which she might have managed to climb over had it not been for her wounded leg. But she was clearly in too much pain to get to her feet, let alone hurdle a fence.

Carlos didn't have to walk very fast to catch up with her.

Once he got there, he strolled alongside her, slowly, as she inched along in the grass, left leg dragging. Looked like the bullet had caught her in the thigh.

"I never slept with him," she said.

Carlos didn't answer. He just shivered.

"Fuck you," she said. She gasped, panted for breath. "Why did you stop Jordan from killing me?"

"No questions, Maggie. We're beyond that now."

"You still love me. You don't want me to die."

"You think?"

"Charlie, you know this is all fucked up. I thought you'd killed your mother. I didn't realise she wasn't in that fucking bodybag. What were you playing at?"

"Me, playing?" He laughed, no humour in it. "How do you know I didn't kill her?"

She looked at him. "Really?"

"Your lack of faith," he said. "It's worse than your infidelity."

"I didn't sleep with Bob. I told you."

"There's more than one way to be unfaithful."

"Do what you have to," she said. "Just don't

66

give me that holier-than-thou bullshit. Shoot me or take me to a hospital. I'm going to bleed to death here."

"Yeah," he said. He bent over, and she shrank away from him. He placed his free hand on the back of her head and lowered his lips to her forehead. "It's over." He stepped back.

"I know."

"I'm sorry."

"I almost believe you."

We need to get moving.

Jordan had walked over to them without Carlos hearing him. Only now did Carlos notice that the kid wasn't wearing shoes. Must have removed them before he got out of the van. Smart little fucker.

"Charlie," Maggie said. "It wasn't me. Your mother. I never set her up."

You going to pop the bitch or what? Jordan said.

Carlos pivoted, smacked Jordan hard, open-handed, with his left. Caught him full on the cheek.

Jordan's head jerked to the side. He waited,

67

breathed, turned to look at Carlos. He looked puzzled.

Carlos stared back at him.

Jordan raised his gun.

Carlos raised his.

Jordan moved his arm to the side, fired two rounds into Maggie.

Carlos's hand shook. He moaned. Couldn't look at Maggie. Couldn't take his eyes off Jordan.

The fucking kid stared at him, blank. Hadn't even turned his gun on Carlos, just let it dangle by his side.

Jordan was daring him. Just like Carlos had done earlier with Bob.

Carlos said, "Is she dead?"

Jordan glanced down. *Very.*

"Jesus," Carlos said. "You fucking little animal. You fucking…" He yelled, mouth wide open, the sides of his mouth stretched fit to tear. He stabbed the gun at Jordan. Looked away, down at Maggie, her ruined body. He yelled again, shoved the gun against Jordan's head, forced him to step back. Carlos took a breath, arm still held out straight, gun a foot from Jordan's face. Spit dribbled down his chin. He wiped it with the back of his left hand, catching a whiff of sour milk.

You done? We need to pick that shit up, get it in the van along with the other one. And get the fuck out of here.

"She's not shit," Carlos said. "You're fucking shit. You're the piece of fucking shit."

You know what? If I could drive, I'd waste you right now. Jordan grabbed Carlos's hand, moved the gun away from his face. *You're a grown man. You need to deal with this.*

***

The little cocksucker was right, of course. Just cause they were in the middle of nowhere at half two in the morning didn't mean no one had heard the shots. Or that a car wouldn't come along and snare them in its headlights.

Carlos needed Jordan's help. He couldn't sort this mess out on his own. There were two bodies now. And only one bodybag. Carlos didn't like numbers that didn't add up.

He lowered his arm. "I'm a bit fucked up," he said.

That's okay. But if you point that gun at me again, I'll have to shoot you. Even if it means I have to walk all the way back home.

Carlos tucked the gun into his waistband, felt the heat still from the muzzle. Felt like it was inside him, glowing.

"You take the feet," he said, shuffled round, slipped his hands under her armpits.

Jordan got into position. *On three, we'll lift it.*

"Her," Carlos said. "We'll lift *her.*"

Fine. You ready?

Yeah, Carlos was as ready as he was going to be.

Wait a minute. Jordan lowered her feet, picked something off the road. Stretched out his hand to offer it to Carlos.

"What is it?"

iPod. Still got the headphones round its — her *— neck, look.*

Carlos took the machine. It looked okay, no cracks that he could see. He slipped the headphones off her neck and put them round his own. He plugged the end into the machine, selected random play and told Jordan to grab her feet again.

Strings. Fiddles and double basses, played posh with a bow. Bach, she'd said. It was supposed to be relaxing.

3

Carlos pulled into a petrol station and got out of the van, checking himself once again for bloodstains. They'd cleaned up with some rags and babywipes that Maggie'd brought along. He'd had a stain on his jumper, probably from Bob, so he'd taken it off. His shoes were pretty bad, and some of the blood had soaked in. But the all-night attendant wasn't going to notice.

Carlos walked over to him, smiled. He hoped the fucker wasn't the talkative type. "Twenty B&H," he said.

The cashier grunted, disappeared to fetch the cigarettes, then returned to the window in his kiosk. He muttered something, presumably the price. Carlos slid a ten-pound note to him, and got his change back with a grunt.

Carlos was about to spring open the packet and light up when he remembered he couldn't do that here.

He walked back to the van, strapped himself into his seat.

You going to smoke in here? Jordan said.

And they'd been getting on so well.

Carlos drove off, looking for a lay-by.

They'd had to get along. Decisions had had to be made. They'd abandoned the idea of chucking the bodies in the Forth. There was only one chain, so they could dispose of one of them that way, but the other was going to be a problem. So they agreed that they'd just dispose of the pair of them with the van. By then, Carlos had been able to think more clearly. It didn't much matter to him whether Maggie had her send-off by water or fire. If anything, fire was the cleaner option. And he was pretty sure it didn't matter to her. He'd need to set up an alibi for himself, but that would be easy enough. And with nothing to link him to the van or the guns, the police wouldn't be able to make a case against him. Not that they'd want to. He was pretty sure it'd be obvious to the dumbest of detectives that he was hurting.

Carlos pulled over. Right under a street-lamp. The sodium light tinted the pavement orange. Or tan.

He lit a cigarette. *Dios*, the smoke bit the back of his throat. He spluttered.

Jordan swore, opened his window.

Carlos took another drag, coughed again. The smoke seeped into his chest, his lungs, and he felt light-headed. Had to be a nicotine rush. Something he hadn't felt since he first started smoking. Or maybe it was adrenaline.

He slipped his headphones on. A bit of Bach and a fag. If that didn't relax him, he was beyond help.

***

Twenty minutes later, they were driving through town, the iPod in the glove box. Carlos fumbled for another fag.

The city was quiet as they coasted down Leith Walk. Jordan opened his eyes when

Carlos sparked the lighter, made a sleepy sound and closed his eyes again.

Carlos's pulse hammered in his temples. He could feel it in his wrists. In the insides of his knees. In the soles of his feet. The nicotine, the adrenaline, Bach, he wasn't sure what or who was to blame.

Jordan was as relaxed as a kitten. *We there yet?* he mumbled.

"Won't be long," Carlos told him. He breathed out a lungful of smoke — felt like he remembered it now, like his body had grown used to the invasion and was at peace with it. He dug out his phone and dialled his mum.

She answered right away.

"Thought you might have fallen asleep," Carlos said.

"As if that's likely. Did you find out what you were after?"

"Maybe," he said.

"Just maybe?"

"I can't talk on the phone."

"How did Maggie take it?"

"Not on the phone, Mama!"

"Okay," she said. "You want me to leave now?"

"Yep. And stay in your car."

This time of night it'd be only a ten-minute drive from here to the patch of wasteland they were headed for. Carlos could have driven for hours like this, the whole city to themselves. He rolled his shoulder, his neck stiff, aware that the prickling inside his head wasn't normal.

***

Carlos cruised along to the stretch of wasteland down by the waterfront. The redevelopment round here was a pain. Hadn't been quite the same since the gasworks were demolished. But it was the best place for the job in hand. This was where joyriders came to burn their rides. He veered off the road, onto scrub and hard dirt, the headlights picking out a straggle of stunted bushes.

He selected his path, turned off the headlights. A few feet on the bumpy terrain and Jordan was jolted awake. Carlos listened to him moan, mutter something about bed.

"We're here," Carlos said, and the kid snapped to it when he realised where they were and that his job wasn't finished yet.

He stretched, shivered, and Carlos eased the van to a stop.

Now? Jordan said.

"Wait till Mum gets here."

Carlos climbed out of the van, the darkness smacking him in the face.

Jordan followed him. He yawned once. *What do you think she'll say?*

Carlos couldn't see Jordan, just heard the voice coming from the other side of the van. Carlos stared at the lonely lights flickering in the distance, wondered what their game was, why they flickered.

Well? When Jordan spoke again, he was just a couple of feet to Carlos's left.

Carlos's hand crept behind his back, fingered the Glock. He could see Jordan now, just, pale face above a shadowy outline. Carlos said, "Why do you care what she'll say?"

Maybe I don't. Just wondering what you'll tell her.

"I don't know," Carlos said. "What should I tell her? Why did you shoot Maggie?"

Can I have one of your cigs?

"Thought you didn't like smoke."

Not in the van. Different outside.

Carlos offered him the packet.

Jordan slid a cigarette out, leaned in for a light.

Carlos lit it, watched Jordan's face glow.

That night, Jordan said, straightening up. *My dad was dying. There was a sword and... the fire...*

"I know," Carlos said. "Richie's dad took a match to the place, right?"

That's what everybody thinks. Not true, though. It was my dad who set the place alight. He paused. *Then he was run through with his own sword. And set on fire by the blaze he started himself.*

"Tough way to go."

That's not how he went.

"No?"

I couldn't let him burn. He sucked on his cigarette, the end glowing. *I shot him.*

Carlos didn't know what to say.

He was in pain. Stabbed through the middle. On fire. I shot him. I stopped the pain.

"Sounds like that was —"

You know how I feel?

"I don't —"

No, you don't. Jordan's glowing cigarette butt arced to the ground, the cigarette not even half-smoked.

"What are you trying to say, Jordan? I'm sorry for what you had to do. But what does it have to do with Maggie?"

Maybe that's your mother. Jordan pointed towards the headlights approaching along the road that led to the waste ground.

"Why Maggie?" Carlos said.

You really have to ask? It needed to be done. And you didn't have the balls to do it yourself.

"She said it wasn't her who'd taken out the contract on my mother."

Maybe, but what about our other dead friend? Bob was there to carry out a contract on you.

"You don't know that."

It's how it looked to me.

"Maggie thought I'd killed my mother."

And that makes it okay?

The car pulled to a stop. "Better check that's Mum," Carlos said. He took out his phone, his thumb stabbing at the phone to light the display.

***

"I can't make out a thing," Carlos's mother said. "Is Maggie there?"

"She left us to it." His mother would find out sooner or later, but Carlos needed to work out what he was going to tell her first. Later was infinitely preferable to sooner. "Not too happy with the stunt we pulled on her."

"Didn't think she would be. How did she get home?"

"I don't know. Probably flagged down a taxi."

"You just let her wander off?"

"Didn't have much choice."

"You spoken to her since?"

"Been too busy."

"I hope she got home okay. Want me to call her?"

"Don't worry about Maggie." Carlos paused. "It wasn't her."

"You mean…?"

"Yeah."

"I didn't think so."

She was always so fucking right.

"Well," Carlos said. "Better get on with this, I suppose. Be with you soon." He hung up, said, "Come on," to Jordan and together they went round to the back of the van. Carlos opened the back doors, removed a can of petrol and set it on the ground. He took a plain white t-shirt, a can of spray paint, a couple of pencil torches and a box of cooking matches out of the hold-all.

He handed the spray paint and a torch to Jordan. "Write something," he said.

What's the point?

"Make the police think it's joyriders."

But once it's burnt, nobody'll be able to read it.

"They will," Carlos said. He remembered what Maggie had told him. Heard her say, "The heat burns the paint into the bodywork or something. Whatever you write, the cops'll be able to read it once the fire's out. So Bob says."

Fuck, that's weird.

"Fire's weird."

Jordan didn't move.

Carlos turned on his torch, shone the beam at him. "You going to get on with it?"

What should I write?

"Use your imagination."

Jordan moved away.

Carlos stuck his torch in his mouth, soaked the t-shirt in petrol.

When he'd finished, he walked over to watch Jordan's handiwork. Jordan had written FIREMEN on the side of the van and was standing staring at it.

He noticed the beam of Carlos's torch, stepped back. *I'm stuck.*

"Suck," Carlos said, around the torch.

No, stuck.

Carlos took the torch out of his mouth. "Suck," he said. "Add 'suck'."

Okay. Jordan shook the can, sprayed out the word. *'Firemen suck.' Sounds a bit lame.*

"Cock," Carlos said. "Add 'cock'."

Nice.

When Jordan had finished, Carlos said, "Beautiful. Now scribble something else on the other side."

Like what?

"I don't fucking know."

Jordan paused for a moment, then disappeared.

"You mind opening that door while you're there?" Carlos said. He opened the driver's side door himself. Apparently that helped get the oxygen flowing. *Thanks, Bob.* Nearly ready. Just had to wait for Jordan to finish his final touch of graffiti. Carlos picked up the petrol can, walked round to the passenger side to join him, and stood back, listening to the *cshh cshhhp* of the paint leaving the canister.

Done, Jordan said, finally, torchbeam directed at his graffiti. He'd written: BOB WAS HERE, placing the joyrider here committing arson rather than out in the country getting shot. Course, his body was in the van, clearly shot. As was Maggie's. But the more there was to confuse the police, the better.

"Inspired," Carlos said. "Chuck the spray can inside."

Jordan tossed the can.

"And your gun."

You think?

"Can't keep it. It's a murder weapon."

Yours too.

Carlos wrenched the gun out of his waistband, lobbed it into the van.

Jordan nodded, threw his in too.

"Out of the way," Carlos said.

He drenched petrol over the seats. Damn stuff stank. Not what you wanted to smell when you'd been up half the night and you'd just started smoking again and you'd had a bellyful of bloodshed. He went round to the back, jumped inside, splashed more petrol around the interior. Splashed it over Bob. Hesitated as the torchlight spilled from his mouth and onto Maggie. It didn't look like her. Not in the least. He poured petrol on it.

The can was feeling much lighter when he heard a voice say, "Oh, my God." The voice came from the darkness outside the van. But it was unmistakably his mother's. *Mierda*. He put down the can. Only then did he twist his head, caught his mother in the narrow beam, hands pressed over her mouth. What the fuck was she doing out of her car?

"Is that a body?" she asked.

It's Maggie. Jordan was suddenly right beside her. *And a friend of hers.*

The little fucker. Carlos clambered out of the van, feet thudded on the ground when he landed.

"Get back in your car, *Mamá*," he said.

"Charlie?"

Carlos rubbed his forehead.

Jordan gave Carlos's mother his torch. *Take a look.*

"Don't do that."

"Let go of me."

Carlos let go of her and she stepped into the van. He grabbed Jordan's arm, steered him away.

"Why are you doing this?" Carlos whispered.

You know what you have to do.

"What the fuck are you saying?"

You haven't worked it out yet?

"The fuck do you mean?"

Your mother. She was the one.

"The one? You mean the one who set herself up? Like fuck she was."

Who else could it have been?

"Could have been anybody."

You don't believe that, though. If you did, you wouldn't have planned what we've done tonight.

"I didn't fucking plan —"

Yeah, yeah, it got a bit fucked up. But you planned on finding out the truth.

"I hoped."

You've just succeeded.

"Suppose I believed you. Why would Mum take out a contract on herself?"

To see how far you would go.

"She didn't know what I did. She had no idea."

Yes, she did.

"How would you know?"

Jordan waited a moment. *Maybe I told her.*

"You don't know her."

Maybe I found out about her.

"How?"

Not so hard.

Carlos thought about the Glock he'd tossed into the front of the van. He shone his torch at Jordan's face, made him blink. "Why would you go to the trouble?"

Squinting. *Because I thought she should know.*

"Nah," Carlos said. "I don't believe you. She was shocked when I told her what I did. She wasn't faking it."

Don't believe me. I don't care. But maybe it's the truth.

"What's the truth?" Carlos's mother said. She stretched out her arms, a gun in each hand. "You shouldn't leave dangerous weapons lying around."

"Mum," Carlos said. "You want to put those down."

"When I'm ready," she said. "They're loaded, I know. I checked. Maggie's dead, Charlie. I really didn't think you'd do it."

"It's not her."

"Charlie."

"It was an accident. Sort of."

"God knows I didn't have a lot of love for her and she certainly had none for me. But, bloody hell, you killed somebody. And not just somebody. You killed your wife."

Carlos looked at Jordan. "Tell her what happened."

Well, Jordan said and started to explain about the police car and Bob and how Maggie had run away and how Carlos had shot her. *In the leg*, he said. *And twice in the body.*

"You little fuck," Carlos said. To his mum: "He's lying. He's the one who shot her."

"Make sense, Carlos," she said.

"He's thirteen years old. He thinks it's fun. That's why he's lying."

"God help you, Carlos."

"I know what it's like to be thirteen. Doesn't take much."

Fuck you, Jordan said. *You know what it's like?* he spat. *Just like you know how I feel? Fuck you. Second half of payment on completion of job. Right, Charlie?* His arm shot out and there was a crack and a flash and Carlos's

88

mother fell to the ground. *Think I wouldn't carry a spare?* He laughed. *I knew you'd get me some piece of shit.*

Carlos switched off his torch, dropped, rolled towards his mother and scrabbled about for one of the guns. His hand touched grass and earth and fabric and skin and something wet and sticky. He retched, just bile, swallowed it down, the taste lingering on his tongue.

He heard Jordan coming towards him.

Carlos's fingers traced down his mother's arm, to her hand. Empty. But right next to it he touched something metal. He grabbed it. Rolled. Turned on the torch.

Jordan was bearing down on him, gun pointed right between his eyes.

Just before Carlos squeezed the trigger, the smell of petrol hit him, and he wondered if there was some on the gun. He wondered if it would light up, the petrol on it igniting. Flames would spread over his hand, a fiery glove. He could feel it blistering his flesh.

But the gun fired its bullet and didn't burst

into flames. Still, his hand felt like it was being held inches from a raging coal fire.

***

Carlos scanned the ground, sweeping the light around in arcs. He spotted the petrol-soaked t-shirt and lobbed it in the van.

He struck a match with his good hand, let it burn, then when the flame had taken hold, he tossed the match onto the t-shirt. The petrol ignited straight away. It was tempting to stay and watch it burn. He had to go, though.

He picked up his mother, slung her over his shoulder.

He ran halfway towards the road before he had to stop for breath. His thighs felt like someone was digging about in them with razor blades.

He looked over his shoulder. Flames leapt into the air. Somebody would spot the fire eventually, get the fire brigade out. But Carlos and his mother would be long gone by then.

They had to go home, get some sleep.

***

He sat his mother up in the car. Fastened her seat belt. The key was in the ignition, or he'd have been fucked.

"Didn't exactly go according to plan, Mum," he said. "Let's get you home. You comfortable?"

I'm fine, he heard her say.

***

He tried not to make too much noise as he entered the house. Didn't want to wake up whatsherface, the babysitter. But it was hard going. His mother was the wrong kind of shape.

He was stinking like a monkey with all the sweat, and the skin on his burnt hand was stinging as the sweat popped through the tender pores. He needed to put something on it. And he would, just as soon as he'd got his mother to bed.

He was dog-tired, his adrenaline spent. He'd shower in the morning.

He laid his mother on the floor while he worked out where to put her.

He opened the sitting room door, peeked inside. The babysitter was on the couch, snoring, a harsh rattle. Maggie had told her she could use the spare room. The girl must have fallen asleep where she was. He wouldn't disturb her now. It was handy, in fact. He could put his mother in the spare room.

The door shut softly and he crept back along the hallway. Had to be careful. Wasn't just the babysitter he didn't want to wake up. Didn't want to wake Sofía either. He gently pushed open the door to her room. Stepped inside. His daughter was snoring too. Ever so lightly, though. Like wind in the trees.

She sounds like you. Maggie's voice, right behind him, her hand on his arm. She squeezed.

"She'll be awake in a couple of hours," he whispered.

Let's take her to bed.

"Don't wake her. Not now." He bent over the cot, smelled the baby sweetness of Sofía's warm head. Kissed her brow. Six months old and he still couldn't believe it. Here lay this little person who would one day call him Daddy.

Come on, Maggie said. *We need to get your mother tucked in.*

***

He ought to have slept soundly—he was tired enough— but sleep wouldn't come. He enjoyed lying there, though, Maggie curled up against him, his baby across the room on the other side of the bed. Pair of them snoring in harmony. Everybody in the house snoring apart from him.

Enjoyed, that is, apart from the images that kept flashing into his head.

Nightmare images. Bob, his thick fingers wrapped around a gun. Maggie dead, a hole in her side. His mother dead, gunshot. So vivid that he put on the light at one stage to check that Maggie was there. She vanished when he turned on the light. He went cold all over for a moment, but it was okay, because he thought of turning off the light and when he did so she came back right away. She told him to go check on his mum. He went through to the spare room and his mum was sound asleep.

He tried to squeeze the unpleasant images

out of his head. They were making him sweat. Making a speeding drumbeat of his heart. And yet when he turned on the light once again, it was enough to soft-focus everything, enough to cushion his brain, enough to skew reality but not so you'd notice straight away. But not for long before he felt the loss of Maggie and he snapped the light off again. A cold fire in his veins.

Maybe there was a gas leak.

Maybe it was the petrol.

His brain was going to rip apart.

Fuck it. There was nothing to worry about.

Forget it. Go to sleep. Listen to the girls snoring.

Forget about the fact you still don't know who wanted your mother dead.

It was Jordan. Had to be. He'd quoted the letter, almost verbatim. Called him Charlie, taunting him. Carlos was as sure as he could be.

But he didn't know for sure and it made him think. Made him worry about what it might mean if it hadn't been Jordan, or Maggie, or his mother. He wasn't accustomed to worrying.

Anxiety. Was that it? Was he having an

anxiety attack? Maybe he should get out of bed, turn on the computer. Look it up, see if the symptoms were — no. That wasn't it. He hadn't experienced any shortness of breath, no pain in the chest. He hadn't felt faint.

He'd just felt… different. Like he was dreaming, even though he knew he was awake. He dreamed he'd shot Jordan. He dreamed he'd burned his hand. He had burned it. The dream was so vivid it made it happen in the real world. Maybe Jordan was dead too.

Carlos got out of bed and walked through to the en-suite and threw up in the sink. This time he didn't hold it back.

***

He must have gone back to bed and fallen asleep because he was jolted awake by a scream. He fumbled around for the light, scrambled out of bed, flung on a dressing gown, opened the door. The babysitter was standing in the doorway of the spare bedroom.

"*Is problemo?*" Carlos said.

She stood there, her head jiggling and her

teeth chattering.

"What?" he said, after a bit.

"On the bed," she said, pointing.

Carlos sighed, padded over to her, peered inside the room. His mother was lying there, fully clothed, sprawled out, on top of the quilt. She didn't look cold or anything, just a little unladylike. "Let her sleep," he said. "She's tired."

"But…" the girl said. "But she's…"

"How much do I owe you?" Carlos said.

"Where's Maggie?"

"She's still asleep."

"Maggie," the girl said, quietly. Then when Maggie didn't appear, she shouted her name.

"How much?" Carlos said.

"I'm getting the fuck out of here." She sprinted for the door, not even bothering to put her shoes on.

Carlos watched her go. Then he went through to the kitchen to get Sofía's feed ready. He'd let Maggie sleep on a bit. It was still early and she'd be tired too. It had been a long night for everyone.